PROJECT POPCORN

by Laura Driscoll
Illustrated by Shirley Ng-Benitez

The Kane Press
New York

For the many volunteers involved every year in the Middletown Community Thanksgiving Project—L.D.

To you, the reader, may the spirit of the Community Champions inspire you!—S. N-B

Acknowledgments: We wish to thank the following people for their helpful advice and review of the material contained in this book: Susan Longo, Former Early Childhood and Elementary School Teacher, Mamaroneck, NY; and Rebeka Eston Salemi, Kindergarten Teacher, Lincoln School, Lincoln, MA.

Special thanks to Susan Longo and Meagan Branday Susi for providing the activities in the back of this book.

Library of Congress Cataloging-in-Publication Data

Names: Driscoll, Laura, author. | Ng-Benitez, Shirley, illustrator.
Title: Project popcorn / by Laura Driscoll ; illustrated by Shirley
    Ng-Benitez.
Description: New York : Kane Press, [2017] | Series: Math matters | Summary:
    The Community Champs learn about the mean, median, mode, average, and
    range as they determine the best way to sell popcorn for a charity
    fundraiser.
Identifiers: LCCN 2016029504 (print) | LCCN 2016047722 (ebook) | ISBN
    9781575658650 (pbk. : alk. paper) | ISBN 9781575658681
Subjects: | CYAC: Fund raising—Fiction. | Average—Fiction. | Business
    mathematics—Fiction. | Mathematics—Fiction.
Classification: LCC PZ7.D79 Pr 2017 (print) | LCC PZ7.D79 (ebook) | DDC
    [E]—dc23
LC record available at https://lccn.loc.gov/2016029504

10 9 8 7 6 5 4 3 2 1

First published in the United States of America in 2017 by Kane Press, Inc.
Printed in China

MATH MATTERS is a registered trademark of Kane Press, Inc.

Visit us online at www.kanepress.com

 Like us on Facebook
facebook.com/kanepress

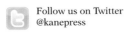 Follow us on Twitter
@kanepress

"Thanks for your order!" William called, waving goodbye to his neighbor.

Yesss. Two more tins of popcorn—SOLD! William couldn't wait for tonight's Community Champions meeting. He could already tell this fundraiser was going to be the best one ever.

That evening at the meeting, William sat next to his friend Lizzie. "I've sold six tins so far!" he whispered to her.

Lizzie looked impressed. "I wonder what this year's badge will look like," she replied.

The Champs
earned a badge
for each volunteer
project they did.
William had one
from cleaning up
the park . . .

one from singing at the
senior center . . .

and one from last year's popcorn fundraiser.
Every year, they gave the popcorn money to a
different charity.

Mr. Cole, the group leader, had an announcement. "This year, we will be raising money for the Thanksgiving Project! They donate large baskets of food—a complete turkey dinner—to families in need."

Mr. C showed them the group's website. The Champs were quiet as they read the messages.

THANKSGIVING PROJECT

Messages from Last Year's Basket Recipients

"When my mom lost her job, we couldn't afford a big Thanksgiving dinner. But we did have one thanks to the Thanksgiving Project!"

"The Thanksgiving Project saved our holiday!"

"It means a lot to know that our community cares about us."

Then Lizzie broke the silence. "The more popcorn we sell, the more families we help!" she exclaimed.

The Champs brainstormed ways to sell more popcorn tins than ever before.

"How have we sold the most tins in other years?" William asked.

Mr. C replied, "I have records of all of our past popcorn sales. Do you and Lizzie want to look through them for ideas?"

William and Lizzie gave Mr. C four thumbs up.

The next day, they spread out all of Mr. C's notes on William's kitchen table.

"Look!" William said. "This graph shows how many tins we each sold over our first weekend of fundraising last year."

"I remember!" said Lizzie. "I sold door-to-door with Kevin."

William nodded. "And I sold with Angie. The other kids set up a popcorn stand outside the grocery store."

	Saturday	Sunday	Total
Lizzie and Kevin	3	8	11
William and Angie	2	3	5
Popcorn stand: Tasha, Joey, Hannah, Luke	12	16	28

"Wow! The kids at the popcorn stand sold 28 tins. That's a lot!" Lizzie pointed out.

"Yeah, but they also had more kids selling," William said. "What we need is the *average* number of tins each kid sold. Then we can see what's better—selling door-to-door or at a stand."

The **mean** is the average of a group of numbers. To find the mean, first add all the values to find their total. Then divide by the number of numbers you added together.

Lizzie added up the total number of tins sold door-to-door over that weekend.

Then she divided that number by the number of kids who sold door-to-door.

$11 + 5 = 16$

$16 \div 4 = 4$

4 tins sold per kid door-to-door

$28 \div 4 = 7$

7 tins sold per kid at the stand

William took the total sold at the popcorn stand and divided it by how many kids were selling there.

"So on *average*," said William, "each kid at the popcorn stand sold more tins than each kid selling door-to-door."

William and Lizzie told the Champs. They agreed to set up popcorn stands every weekend. One stand would be at the park, and one outside the grocery store.

At their first sale, they had lots of customers! Toward the end of the sale, a woman came up to buy three tins of the Kettle Corn flavor.

But the box of Kettle Corn tins was empty. They'd already sold out!

"Oh, well," the woman said. "That's my favorite flavor."

"Sorry!" William said as the woman walked away. "We'll have more next weekend!"

We lost out on a sale! thought William. How could he make sure that didn't happen again?

At home, William took another look at Mr. C's notes. He saw that Kettle Corn was always their bestseller.

William made a list. He wrote down how many tins of Kettle Corn they'd sold over each weekend the year before.

One Saturday, they had sold 15 tins. Another day, they'd only sold 7.

But on *most* days, they had sold 10.

The **mode** is the value that is repeated more often than any other number in a list. On the list of Kettle Corn tins sold, the mode is 10.

"So we should always bring at least 10 tins of Kettle Corn," he told Mr. C the next weekend. "And one day last year, we sold *more* than 10. Let's bring a few extra, just in case!"

That day, they brought 15 tins of Kettle Corn.
They sold 13 of them!

Mr. C had big news for the Champs at their next meeting. "This will be the last weekend of the popcorn fundraiser," he told them. "So far, we have sold 175 tins of popcorn!"

The kids cheered. "That's more than we've ever sold before!" said William.

Angie raised her hand. "Let's try to sell everything we have left!" she exclaimed.

"Yeah!" cried Lizzie. "Every tin we sell helps those families. But tins we *don't* sell do nothing."

"Could we lower the price?" suggested Tasha.
William spotted a flyer on a bulletin board.
"Like an Everything Must Go sale!" William said.

They all liked that idea. But what should the
new price be?

"It can't be *too* low," William said after the
meeting. "We still want to raise lots of money!"

Lizzie nodded. "But it has to be low enough
to be a good deal."

They did some research at the store. William wrote down the prices of all the popcorn brands they could find. They compared them to the price of the Champs' popcorn . . . which turned out to be the most expensive.

Store popcorn:
$3.50
$4.00 ← highest
$2.99
$2.25
$2.00 ← lowest
$3.00
$3.95
Champs popcorn:
$5.00

For any list of numbers, the **range** is the difference between the highest value and the lowest value in the list. The range of popcorn prices at the store is $2.00.

$4.00 - $2.00 = ($2.00) range

On the last day of the sale, they set their new price right in the middle of the store prices. It turned out to be just right!

Arrange a group of numbers in order. The number in the middle is called the **median**. In William's list of store popcorn prices, the median is $3.00.

$2.00 $2.25 $2.99   ($3.00) $3.50 $3.95 $4.00

The Champs started out with 45 tins.
In the first hour alone, they sold 15.
In the second hour, they sold 20 more!
By lunchtime, the last tin was gone. "We did it!" William cheered. "We sold out!"

"I'm so proud of all of you," Mr. C told them at the next meeting. He was passing out the new badges they had earned.

William looked at his. He had the perfect spot for it on his sash.

"Mr. C?" William asked. "How many families do you think will get a Thanksgiving basket this year?"

Mr. C smiled. "I don't know," he replied. "But I know how we can find out!"

The day before Thanksgiving, the whole group was at Thanksgiving Project headquarters. They were helping to pack all the baskets. "There are so many!" William said to Lizzie.

A volunteer overheard them. "There are 200!" she told them. "That's double what we gave away last year. Your donation really helped with that!"

William beamed. The following day, all those families would be sitting down to a big turkey dinner. They might not have had one without help from the Champs.

That was a pretty good feeling.

It felt even better a few weeks later when they got some very special mail. Mail giving thanks for Thanksgiving.

The Mendozas
21 East Main St. #2
San Jose, CA 95103

The Community Champions
North Avenue

Happy Thanksgiving!

To the Champions

It was a happy holiday thanks to you!

—The Robinsons

MEAN, MEDIAN, MODE, AND RANGE

The **mean** is the average of a group of numbers. To find the mean, add up all the numbers in a group and then divide that sum, or total, by how many numbers there are in the group.

Example: 15, 20, 15, 10
Add the *four* numbers together. 15 + 20 + 15 + 10 = 60
Divide the sum by *four*. 60 ÷ 4 = 15
The **mean** is 15.

The **median** is the middle number in a list of numbers that are arranged in order.

Example: 10, 15, 20, 25, 30, 35, 40, 45, 50
The number in the middle is 30.
The **median** is 30.

The **mode** is the number that appears most frequently in a group of numbers.

Example: 25, 32, 68, 25, 78, 25, 65, 14
The number that appears most often is 25.
The **mode** is 25.

The **range** is the difference between the highest and lowest numbers in a group. In other words, it's the highest number *minus* the lowest number.

Example: 1, 7, 9, 3, 2, 4
9 (highest) – 1 (lowest) = 8
The **range** is 8.